THE DIVINER

Retold and illustrated by
Joyce Audy dos Santos

J. B. Lippincott   New York

Designed by Al Cetta

1 2 3 4 5 6 7 8 9 10

First Edition

Library of Congress Cataloging in Publication Data

dos Santos, Joyce Audy.
The diviner.

SUMMARY: A lazy but clever lad earns, through shrewd guesswork and luck, the reputation of being a diviner.
[1. Folklore, French Canadian] I. Title.
PZ8.1.D748Di 1980   398.2'1'09714   [E]   79-9616
ISBN 0-397-31909-6
ISBN 0-397-31910-X (lib. bdg.)

to Mémère Rose,
with love

Jean-Pierre was very lazy. People said, "Why, he is so lazy, he won't even swat a fly from his own nose."

Now Jean-Pierre was clever as well as lazy. He could finagle his way out of any bit of work at all.

When the time came for him to make his own way in the world, he couldn't imagine himself feeding pigs or plowing fields. Instead, he decided to live off his wits. "I will be Jean-Pierre the Diviner," he declared. "I can solve riddles and foretell the future as well as anyone."

He made a placard to advertise himself and drifted off in search of an easy fortune.

His fee was to be one night's lodging. First he correctly guessed that the miller's pregnant wife would at last have a boy. Then he advised a shepherd whose entire flock had been carried off by a marauding wolf that finally the beast would not return. So, encouraged by his luck, he grew bolder.

As he traveled along in the lazy man's way, looking for his next meal, he came to a castle.

By the gate stood the King. "Good day, Jean-Pierre," he called.

"A good day to you, Sire," Jean-Pierre replied.

"Are you really able to divine the answer to any question?" asked the King.

"Try me," said Jean-Pierre.

"The Queen's favorite ring is missing," said the King. "My servants have scoured every corner and crack for it. The wisdom of all my advisors with their countless degrees and titles has been applied to the problem. Still the ring has not been found."

"Aha!" thought Jean-Pierre. "My luck improves with age."

"Before I can divine the solution to such a difficult problem," he told the King, "I must be in the proper mood. I need just the right atmosphere. Provide for me a comfortable room and three good meals each day, and at the end of three days I will have the answer."

Now he had secured three days of easy living, but what of the ring? "Oh, I'll surely think of something," he promised himself.

Jean-Pierre was shown to a magnificent room with leaded windows, a mosaic floor, and tapestried walls—a room fit for one with such an awesome talent as Jean-Pierre claimed to have. The King ordered three of his servants to care for the visitor's needs.

At breakfast, the first servant brought the Diviner a tray of tasty pastries, and later a lunch of succulent meats. As the servant was leaving the room after bringing a hearty dinner, he overheard something. Jean-Pierre, his belly full of warm food, had been thinking of his three days of comfort. He said aloud, "Now one has passed, soon the other two will follow."

The servant scurried to the kitchen in terror. "He knows all about us!" he cried to the others. You see, it was these three who had taken the ring. The guilty servant thought Jean-Pierre meant that he had seen one thief and that two remained. "The King will have our heads now for sure!" he wailed.

"Stop raving and listen," said the second servant. "This story is all nonsense. You don't really believe the words written on that placard, do you? Tomorrow I will serve him, and I think I will hear nothing."

So, on the second day the second servant smoothed his moustache, straightened his jacket, and brought Jean-Pierre his three satisfying meals. The servant heard nothing to alarm him. As he opened the door to carry away the dinner dishes, he thought that certainly the first servant had worried over nothing.

Jean-Pierre sat wondering what he would tell the King. Two of his three days were gone, and he was no closer to finding the Queen's ring. To the servant's horror, the Diviner mused, "Now two have passed, soon the third will follow."

Like a dog with his tail on fire, the servant raced to the kitchen.

"We're doomed!" he cried.

"Do you think the Diviner would help us if we gave him the ring?" suggested the third servant.

"It's our only hope," replied the first. And so they agreed.

The next day the third servant waited on the Diviner. Jean-Pierre was worried. His third day was almost gone.

With dinner tray in hand, the servant was leaving the room when the Diviner said, "Now all three have passed."

The servant rushed back to Jean-Pierre and cringed at his feet. "You know we took the ring!" he cried.

Sly Jean-Pierre felt that good luck was smiling down upon him once more.

"Of course I know," he replied.

"Oh, please don't tell the King," whined the servant. "Here, please find a way to give it back."

Jean-Pierre, the rascal, agreed.

"You must be very wise," the servant went on. "The King's advisors were baffled, but you uncovered us as easily as if I had told you myself!"

"Just as you say," answered Jean-Pierre.

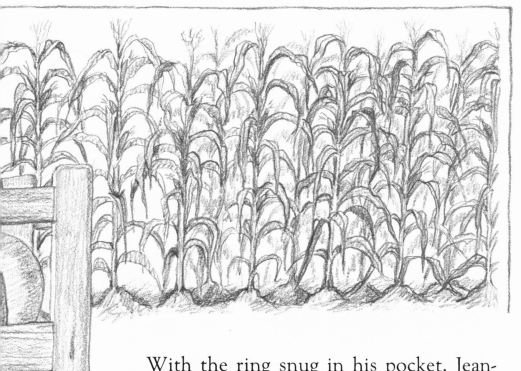

With the ring snug in his pocket, Jean-Pierre went to meet the King. "Sire, one more thing," he said.

"What is it?" the King asked impatiently.

"I would like to see more of your estate," answered Jean-Pierre.

The King proudly took Jean-Pierre on a tour of the royal gardens, the stable, and the pens for the livestock. When the King turned to point out his fine pigs, Jean-Pierre tossed the ring toward a group of hungry-looking turkeys. The plumpest one gobbled it right up.

Presently the King said, "You have seen
all that I own. Now tell me, where is the
ring?"

"You will find it," the Diviner confident-
ly replied, "in that big turkey over there."

"Impossible!" said the King. "How could
the turkey have the Queen's ring?"

"Sire, my life is in your hands if the ring is
not in that turkey," answered wily Jean-
Pierre.

The King thought that was absurd. But
he had the Diviner's word, so he ordered the
turkey killed.

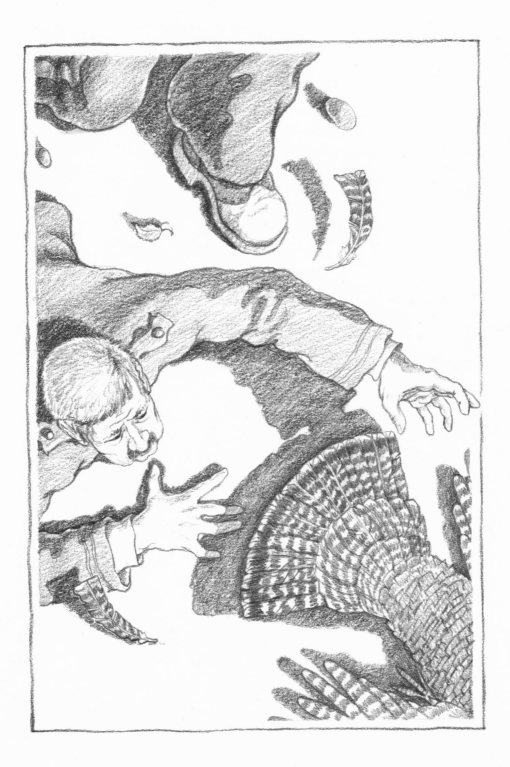

The ring, of course, was found inside. The King was delighted. He invited the Diviner to stay longer, but now Jean-Pierre was in a curious hurry to leave. Three days of luxury richer, he didn't want to turn his luck.

The King insisted on walking him to the gate. He was reluctant to let Jean-Pierre go and couldn't resist making one last test. He covered with his cap three hickory nuts that were by the side of the path. "Just a minute," he called ahead to Jean-Pierre. "Tell me, what do I have under my cap?"

Now Jean-Pierre knew he couldn't possibly guess what was under the King's cap. But he was already standing safely outside the castle walls. So he scornfully shouted, "Oh, nuts!"—then turned and ran.

AUTHOR'S NOTE

As a child Rose Robidoux was amused by a story, told to her in her native French, called "Le Divineur." Originally from Warwick, Quebec, her family moved to the United States where she worked in the textile mills, married, and eventually had seven children. "Le Divineur" was among the stories she told, complete with the appropriate facial expressions and gestures, to her delighted family. Her story hours were open to some of the neighborhood children, who would hurry through their homework so they could come after supper and listen enthralled to story after lively story. So real did she make those tales seem that she still, in her eighties, chuckles over the awestruck faces of her audience.

Rose Robidoux is my grandmother. She has told me "The Diviner" in English, and my children have heard it too. Now I am passing it on in my own way, and although I've adjusted it here and there to fit into book form, it is still "Le Divineur."